Text Copyright 2004 by Anne Margaret Lewis
Illustration Copyright 2004 by Kathleen Chaney Fritz

First Edition

Library of Congress Cataloging-in-Publication Data

Lewis, Anne Margaret and Chaney Fritz, Kathleen
Tears of Mother Bear
Summary: As Grandpa walks the shores of Lake Michigan with his grandchildren he passes on the age old Ojibwe Sleeping Bear legend, and reveals the untold story of where Petoskey stones come from.
They are the tears of mother bear.
ISBN 0-9749145-0-9
Fiction

10 9 8 7 6 5 4 3 2 1

Printed and bound in Canada by Friesens, Altona, Manitoba.

A Mackinac Island Press, Inc. publication

For my four children, Caitlin, Matthew, Patrick and Cameron
who are my most precious of gifts.

Anne Margaret Lewis

To my son Christopher, thank you for letting me relive childhood through your eyes,
reminding me that life is as innocent and fun as you want it to be.

Kathleen Chaney Fritz

As summer was fast approaching
And school was coming to an end
I'd be dreaming of summer vacation
Of traveling to our cottage once again

Our cottage was right next to Grandpa's
On the edge of the big, big lake
It's known as great Lake Michigan
Sandy beaches, rock hunting,
   and sand castles we'll make

Our favorite way to pass the time
Is to take our daily stroll
With Grandpa as our rock-picking guide
We walk the squeaky sand,
    scrunching our toes

Grandpa had a name for each and
    every stone:
Christmas rocks, Saturn rocks,
    and salt and pepper ones too
"Look Grandpa, what's this clear blue rock?"
    I asked.
Grandpa replied, "I call that baby blue."

"What do you call these flat rocks, Grandpa?"
He said, "The skinny ones are known
    as skippers."
"What about this spoon-shaped gray rock?"
Grandpa laughed and said,
    "Hey, that's the big dipper."

We'd skip the skippers from wave to wave
One, two, three, four or more times they'd skip
As they'd hit the water one last time
"Look Grandpa, mine's doing a flip."

"I found one, I got one, hey look over here!"
Grandpa yelled from afar,
"A Petoskey stone, I finally found one."
I replied, "Hey, let's take it home in a jar."

"No!!" Grandpa shrieked, "You mustn't."
"You must kiss it and throw it
    back in the lake.
Petoskeys are the most precious of stones,
They are the tears of Mother Bear,
    for goodness sake."

Petoskeys are many shades of gray
They're a beautiful six-sided design
When the water washes them
    clean from sand
They sparkle, and shimmer, and shine

Then, Grandpa pointed to Mother Bear
As she laid above the great sand dune
That dropped into deep Lake Michigan
All dressed in a brilliant blue

He reminded us of the story of Sleeping Bear
How Mother Bear tried to save her cubs
How she waited and waited for them to swim to safety
With her never-ending love

As Grandpa continued to tell the story
We saw a little tear
Just like the tears of Mother Bear
They were tears of joy, not fear

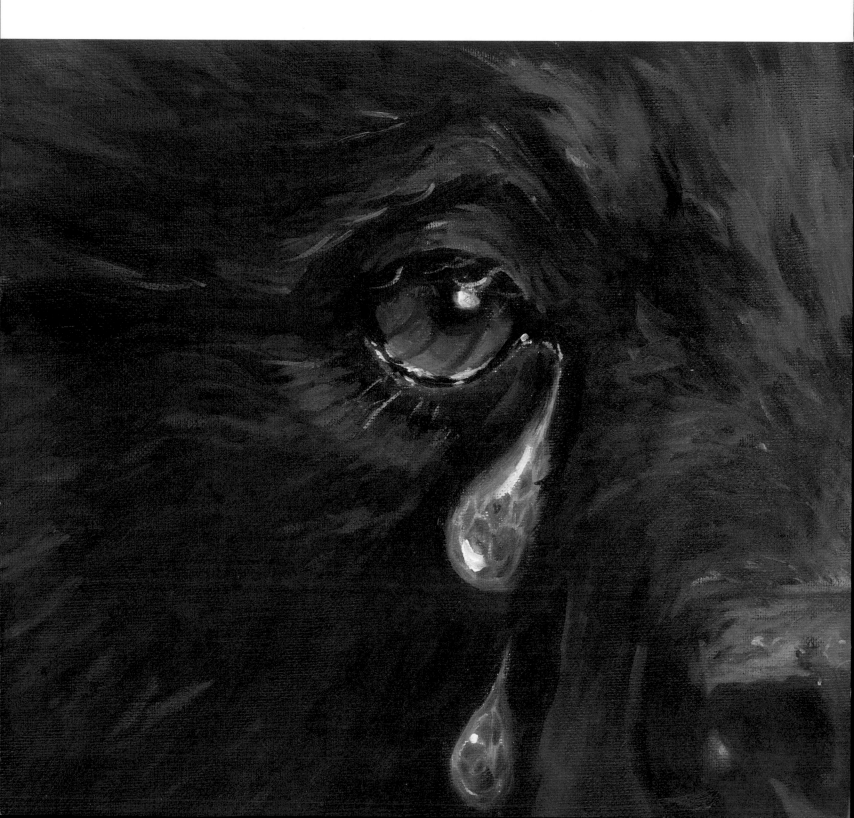

Grandpa ended the story
of how the little cubs
Were reunited with Mother Bear
As little islands of love

Mother Bear lay above the
    Sleeping Bear Dunes
Keeping a watchful eye
Crying her tears of happiness and joy
And breathing a deep, deep sigh

Her tears continued to roll
    down the dune
Into the lake that never ends
And when they reach her baby cubs
It's a message of love she sends

Grandpa says when the tears reach the cubs
    they kiss each one
Then send them back into the lake
Only then can the great
    waves of Lake Michigan
Wash them back to Mother Bear;
    not for us to take

Each time when we're out rock hunting
We look for Mother Bear's tears
We look for the great Petoskey stone
and when we find one, we let out a happy cheer!

We know when we find a Petoskey stone
We have love and joy in our lives
Just like the tears of Mother Bear
The love of her cubs survives

We know summer vacation has come to an end
When the glow of the sun sets so early
"We'll rock hunt next summer on Lake Michigan shores
To find Mother Bears tears," Grandpa says surely.

As we waved him goodbye, we let out a sad sigh
For we watched and we knew he'd be waiting
Just as Mother Bear had for her cubs long ago
With a Petoskey in hand, he stood waving